The Colorways of Time

Book One: The Three Kingdoms

Written by Marc Eliot

Illustrations by Theresa Giannone

Acknowledgements

Thank you to my remarkable parents Elaine and Gil, who gave me the happiest childhood imaginable. I owe my drive, creative mind and finding all my passions to you both. And to all of the children in my life who share their funny, inspired, wise, and unbridled imaginations with me each and every day. Thank you for keeping my life filled with timeless adventure.

I am most grateful to my wife Toby for her love and constant support. Thank you for being my editor, proofreader, and sounding board. But most of all, thank you for being my biggest fan and best friend.

To Theresa Giannone who illustrated the book. Thank you for always understanding my conceptual visions and bringing them to life.

To Mary Ellin Kurtz and Marla Siegel thank you for all your help in getting my creative adventure on to paper and making Colorways possible.

Contents

Contents

Chapter 1 The Clouds

The enchanted garden was a warm oasis nestled within an otherwise frozen region. It was alive with white doves circling a glade of glistening trees bearing sumptuous gilded fruits. A pink and gold glow shimmered from deep within the garden, giving it warmth and life.

Teragil, an ancient man with wise eyes and a smile that hinted of truths untold, sat by the edge of the garden's sparkling stream. Jalek was a twelve-year-old-boy who described things he liked as "cool" or "nice." Had he seen the magical places the older man described, he might have even called them beautiful.

At least that's what Teragil assured the young boy, and since he'd been the one to see all this in person, Jalek was inclined to believe him. Teragil was old, far older than Jalek's parents or even his Grandpa G, who walked with a cane and spent a lot of time telling stories about life "back when." Teragil told a lot of stories too, but they were different. Grandpa G's experiences didn't seem out of the ordinary, while Teragil's tales were exciting and told by a man who seemed to have loved every one of what Jalek figured had to be over a million days on the planet.

"When I was a young one like you, Jalek, there were three kingdoms. The first kingdom, Gloriosa, was a magical city in the clouds, floating on the edge of heaven and space. The fluffy clouds went on for eternity. Streams of soft pale light in yellows, oranges, and pinks joined the clouds together. Forests of towering melaph trees with musical liquid leaves swayed in the gentle breeze. Thousands of glowing butterfly birds called flurbur danced overhead, their beating wings creating a gentle musical sound. The kingdom was protected by flocks of white doves and at the horizon, beautiful white horses flew to protect the outer perimeters.

"Queen Shaana ruled Gloriosa. Shaana was a breathtaking young woman with bright emerald eyes and golden brown hair that shimmered to her fingertips. Her smile was as light as the sunrise. She was as kind as she was beautiful and ruled Gloriosa with wisdom and grace. Like many with a great deal of power and responsibility, deep inside she worried about whether she would successfully live up to everyone's expectations. Could she serve and protect the people who relied on her? Assisting Shaana and making her burden easier to bear were Recima, a young girl wise beyond her years and Gaba, a good-natured boy whom everybody adored.

"The people lived in peace among the clouds in their kingdom. The streets were flowing streams, and the people walked across them on paths of stones. Music was an important part of life on Gloriosa. It could be heard throughout the kingdom, from the melaph leaves that softly rang like windchimes, from the fluburs' fluttering wings and from the people singing. The most interesting sounds of all came from the little sparkling crystals in the street streams, which made lyrical piano-like sounds. No one knew where the crystals came from, because the streams weren't cold enough to make such icy crystals."

"But wasn't it noisy with all that music?" asked Jalek. "Didn't people complain about it being too loud?"

Teragil smiled. "Oh, no, Jalek, it was the most enchanting sound in the entire universe. There were places all along the streams where people sat to eat the delicious fruit of the setre trees, drink the fresh mint-water from the streams, and make music. The serenity of the music and the beauty of the cloud kingdom made the people there smile more often than you see back home."

"Were there children in Gloriosa?" Jalek asked.

"Of course," replied the Ancient One. "There were many young ones just like you. They played games that you'd enjoy. One was Cometball – you'd reach into the nearest cloud and pull out some cloudfluff. Then you'd pack it into a ball, and when you threw it, glowing orange tails flew out behind the ball as it sailed through the air."

"Cool!" said Jalek, who loved all sorts of sports, including the ones he'd never even played or wasn't especially good at. "What else?"

Teragil paused, digging through the world's largest memory archives to provide further examples. "Well, in another game, you'd make a cloudball and tap it with the back of your fingers. The softer you'd tap, the higher the cloudball would go. But if you tapped it too hard, the cloudball stayed on your fingers. Most of the older children played Fabasclou. Two teams rode bubbles and tried to get a Cometball through a moving hoop, and on to a goal at the ends of the playing field. The goals moved opposite the hoop and the game was won when a team got the Cometball through the hoop and the goal together."

"How else were things different there?" Jalek wanted to know.

"Everywhere you looked, a gentle mist flowed up from the clouds, with sunrays streaming through. The mist and sun together created energy for the kingdom, which was stored in the clouds and made them glow a soft pastel shade. Arching colorways connected all the clouds, and people traveled on the colorways in bubbles of energy to move throughout the kingdom. When you looked far off in the misty distance, castles with tall spires rose in the clouds. People lived in the castles and nearby cottages, which all twinkled in the soft sunlight. Fruit trees and waterfalls surrounded every home and the white doves fluttered above with flying horses even higher up in the sky. It was a truly magical place," Teragil concluded, smiling at the memories.

"Is Gloriosa still there? Can we go?" asked Jalek.

"All in good time, young one," laughed the Ancient One.

"Remember I said there were three kingdoms? Don't you want to hear about the others?"

"Sure," Jalek said, remembering the teacher who had recently told him that he needed to be a more attentive listener.

"The second kingdom, called Polara, was a mysterious opposite of Gloriosa. It too was a kingdom in the clouds, but everything that was light and bright in Gloriosa was dark and without color in Polara. It was gray and cold and even the clouds that hung over the kingdom seemed brittle and frozen. Sunlight didn't penetrate the high clouds, though from afar Polara had an aura that was very unique.

"Queen Tala ruled Polara. In her youth she had beauty and grace that matched Shaana's, but she had become bitter. Because there was no sunlight or warmth, the people in Polara looked old and withered, most of the trees were barren of fruit, and the streams were either dry or choked with ice. Deep within this kingdom was a place where everything was frozen. The ice people who lived in the Frozen Zone were pale and covered with icicles. Trunkleskunkles, which were frozen trees, came to life briefly when anyone passed nearby. But Polara hadn't always been that way. Many years ago, it had been as warm and beautiful as Gloriosa.

"So what happened to Polara that changed it?" Jalek wanted to know.

"Ah, that's where our tale begins…" said Teragil. "A thousand years before this, there was only one kingdom in the clouds, full of light and life."

"And that was Gloriosa?" Jalek asked.

"Yes, that's correct, How very clever of you," Teragil replied, noticing that Jalek looked embarrassed but pleased to receive the compliment.

"Kier and Tala were the young king and queen, and Shaana was their sweet little girl. Like most little girls she was unsure of herself, yet she had the ability to make those around her feel special.

Like all Gloriosans, Kier and Tala loved exploring their cloud kingdom. On one trip, they came to a high point on a cloud overlooking all of time and space. It was a magical place where flurbur fluttered between the musical leaves of the melaph trees. They noticed a glistening colorway leading to a new cloud formation that they hadn't seen before, which wasn't at all unusual in a kingdom made of everchanging clouds where there was always something new to discover. Kier and Tala crossed the colorway and followed a long winding path into a hidden forest. They were the only people who had chosen this particular path. They came to a misty glade and found a sparkling pool and waterfall that appeared to glow.

They were fascinated by the glow and discovered that it emanated from behind the waterfall. While Tala waited by the edge of the pool, Kier stepped into the cool water and discovered a glowing emerald stone behind the waterfall. Although he didn't know it, he and Tala were the only Gloriosans with the power to see the stone, which was a key that opened the portal to another world.

He picked up the stone, but as he turned to bring it back to Tala, he slipped and found himself falling through space with no control over where he was going or whether he'd ever return.

Chapter 2 Polara

Jalek jumped up from his seat. He was an energetic boy who struggled to sit still for long periods of time, especially given that Teragil's story had taken an exciting turn. "What happened to Kier?"

Teragil looked thoughtfully at Jalek before answering. "Kier tumbled and turned through layer after layer of clouds and space. He landed on what he thought was a cloud in the lower part of the kingdom. The impact knocked him into a deep sleep. He awoke a long time later and slowly sat up, stiff and sore from the hard landing. He looked around, but nothing looked familiar. The colors were strange and harsh, and the land was hard and dry."

"Where was he?" Jalek asked. He couldn't imagine what it would feel like to plummet through space, whether he'd be scared or excited or some combination of both.

"It turned out to be a kingdom called Marinus," Teragil replied.

"So what happened to Tala?"

"Well, when Kier removed the stone and fell through the portal, a thunderous rumble shook Gloriosa. When the cloud kingdom shuddered, Tala was tossed down beside the waterfall.

Although the sun shone brightly, the colorway that Tala and Kier had crossed over to reach the new cloud was slowly fading. Tala knew that if the colorway between the clouds disappeared, she wouldn't be able to find her way back to the castle where Shaana was waiting. Tala and the others ran as fast as their legs would carry them toward the dimming colorway. Some crossed it safely back, but others were stranded in the middle as it faded beneath them, and they fell into oblivion. Just as Tala reached the colorway, it vanished. At that moment, Gloriosa was severed in two."

"And the part Tala was still standing on became Polara," guessed Jalek.

"You're exactly right," Teragil said approvingly. "And from that time on, there have been three kingdoms."

"I've never even seen one kingdom," Jalek said wistfully. "Unless you count the Magic Kingdom at Disneyland."

"You may see a real kingdom one day, Jalek. One never knows what the future might bring. The residents of Polara and Gloriosa were uncertain about their futures as well. At first, Polara and Gloriosa were very much alike. Both were warm, sunny, and colorful. But with the colorway gone, Polara slowly drifted away from Gloriosa. Dark clouds began forming overhead and stayed for many weeks. Without the sun's light and warmth, everything in Polara faded. What had been a vibrant place slowly turned gray and cold. While the clouds were heavy and dark, they provided very little rain, so the trees and plants withered. As Polara grew colder, the people withered too.

"Tala was desperately lonely without Shaana and Kier and missed them more as each day passed. For years, she and Kier had spent most of their waking hours by each other's sides. Without his energy and his ability to turn even the most grim situation into an exciting adventure, she felt lost. In addition to missing Kier, she blamed herself for causing Polara's break from Gloriosa. She felt that if only she had kept Kier from taking the stone behind the waterfall, he wouldn't have fallen through the portal, and this trouble and misery might have been avoided. Now, she was forever separated from the two people she loved most in the cosmos. The thought of never seeing them again gradually turned her into a cold and bitter woman."

Jalek cringed. "I thought this was an adventure story, not a love story."

Teragil smiled. "Love can be quite an adventure. One day you may discover that yourself."

"Never," Jalek said, though maybe not quite as adamantly as he would have a couple of years ago.

"Anyway, Teragil, I don't understand why Polara changed. And why did the colorway between Polara and Gloriosa disappear in the first place?"

"It was the stone, my boy - the magical emerald stone. It provided energy and power in Gloriosa. As new clouds developed, the stone generated new colorways to connect them. Remember that Kier and Tala were the only ones who could see the stone glowing. It had always been there behind the waterfall, but only they had the power to see and use it. When Kier fell through the portal with the stone in his hand, he removed the power source for the colorway, and in that moment changed the history of the three kingdoms."

"But if the magical stone was the power source, why didn't Gloriosa turn cold and gray like Polara?" Jalek asked.

"Maybe the stone was not the only source of power," hinted Teragil.

The boy pondered this for a long time.

Then it came to him: "There was another stone on the Gloriosa side of the color-way!"

"Yes, there were two."

Chapter 3 Frozen Time

"You said there were three kingdoms," Jalek reminded him. "What was the third?"

"Deep within Polara, on the other side of the waterfall where the stone used to be, was a mysterious place. Everything there was covered in crystallized ice. The Spirited Ones of Polara named Rezak, Albee, and Azeal, had discovered this frosty terrain. They were the only ones who could navigate through this fascinating world."

"They must have been cold and scared," said Jalek.

Teragil's reply surprised him. "Not at all. In fact, the Spirited Ones were determined to understand what was happening and why. One day early in the morning, they set out to discover the secret of the Frozen Zone. Remember where Kier found the stone?"

"Yes," said Jalek, rather proud of himself for knowing the answer. This was a much easier story to pay attention to than the ones Mrs. Landingham read aloud to them at school.

"By the waterfall!"

"That's right! Well, the Spirited Ones found themselves at the foot of the waterfall. A faint glow appeared behind the falling cascade. As they stepped through the water, all three slid down this slippery slope. Tumbling through a blizzard of fog and blowing white powder, they landed at the foot of an ice covered forest: The Frozen Zone. It was filled with towering trees covered in fine white powder. Their branches were crystallized in ice, yet the leaves quivered with movement.

Extraordinary creatures of both sky and land inhabited this frosty corridor. The birds all seemed frozen, but yet they could soar among the limbs of the frozen trees. The trees were 'alive'!"

"I don't understand," said Jalek. "How can frozen trees be alive?"

"Remember," said Teragil, "it was a mysterious place, and the magical happenings there can't be explained with science and logic."

"I understand," said Jalek, and he was pretty sure he did.

"As the birds came to rest on the trees, they became the limbs; their icy feathers, the leaves. By now, the Spirited Ones were fascinated, awed, and a little bit frightened by this frosty, glistening place. As they looked behind them, they could not find the place from which they came.

Rezak decided to move forward and explore. Albee and Azeal followed, somewhat reluctantly – "It's too cold!" they said. Like you, my young friend, they didn't embrace the cold. But onward they went, and they kept going even when it seemed they might not succeed. What seemed like days later, tired and hungry, they saw something in the distance. It appeared to be a white dove circling over what looked like a pond. As they approached, they could see that, in fact, it was a pond of fresh water, and the white dove was leading them straight to it. They saw that the dove actually had a face, the face of a child. She told them her name was Becca Hall. She was a Seer: a timeless being. She created this oasis with powers never seen before.

She told them the age-old tale of how the Frozen Zone came to be and that their help was needed to stop it from engulfing all of Polara. She told the story of Kier falling through the portal and how Polara came to be. In order to save Polara, they would have to make their way to the core of the Frozen Zone. There they would find the secret, the key to reunifying the kingdoms: a way of transcending time. Without their help, the ice age would take over Polara as well as Gloriosa."

"Oh no," cried Jalek. "What'd they do next? And what about Kier? And..."

Teragil assured him that all his questions would be answered in good time.

Chapter 4 Marinus

Kier awoke and realized he was not only in a strange place, but a new world. He began to explore. Behind him were immense trees and unusual birds soaring through the air. Above the cliffs were mountains that seemed to stretch on forever above a vast sea. Truly, this was a special place.

"He was on Marinus, wasn't he?" asked Jalek.

"That's right," Teragil answered. "The blue-green sea amazed him. It was nothing like he had ever encountered before! He climbed down the edge of the cliff to where the water touched the land. There, in the water, were these tiny wondrous creatures."

"Fish!" said Jalek.

"Putting his foot in the water, he smiled, and began to move through it. The sun on his face encircled him in warmth and comfort; he felt young again! Kier was not accustomed to being alone. All his life, he had been surrounded by people of the kingdom and by Tala, his true love. He missed her even more than he would let himself realize. As he looked up at the clear blue sky, he pictured her face before him and wondered how he'd ever survive without her. When Kier became aware of his surroundings again, he realized he was on a piece of land with water on all sides."

"An island," deduced Jalek.

"That's right," said the Ancient One. "And instead of allowing himself to think more about Tala, he focused on more practical concerns. This ability to put aside fear long enough to formulate a plan had always served him well as king. After floating back to shore, he found he was hungry. What he hadn't yet figured out was how he would eat."

"He could catch fish," suggested Jalek.

"You're right, but he needed to find that out on his own. As the sun set, the wind began to blow. Huge black clouds blotted out the sun's rays. The sea grew dark, and angry and wind-whipped waves crashed at his feet. There was a rumble in the distance and streaks of light shot across the otherwise darkened sky. Drops of water fell from the heavens, harder and ever faster. Kier, having never seen a thunderstorm, was awed by nature's power. Behind a grove of windswept trees, he found a cave where he waited out the storm.

As the storm passed, he saw a glow in the distant night sky. A large shadow was cast across the sea. At the outer boundaries of the world along the ocean line stood the guardians of the colorways. Enormous robotic figures majestically rising from the water. There they would always remain, radiating a glow and protecting the colorways of time. Keep this in mind, my young friend, just as Kier survived by learning about the world around him, you too might one day benefit from this information and knowledge."

Chapter 5 Frozen in Time

It was as if the whole world stood still. The Frozen Zone was a place without motion or sound.

Nonetheless, if you stood still and paid close attention, you could detect faint signs of life. Crystal globes of glass radiated a blue glow from within. Moss of a metallic nature glistened on the crystalized trees that stretched high in the air.

"Wait!" yelled Jalek. "What happened to Kier? What is this place? Is it the North Pole?"

"Have patience, my young friend," advised the Ancient One. "Soon you will understand. Remember I referred to three kingdoms? A long time ago, before Gloriosa, this was all there was. Dramatic ivory landscapes and mountains that stretched beyond the sky. The reflection of sparkling ice went beyond the horizon and as far as the eye could see."

"That's a lot of ice," Jalek said, and this observation brought a smile to the old man's face.

"You have a magnificent gift for understatement. Now, remember I told you of the towering trees and the frozen birds that could fly?"

"Yes," replied Jalek, who was listening more attentively than he ever did in school.

"Well, the birds were called frozibs. In the most remote part of this kingdom, high atop the tallest tree, enormous globes of glass shimmered at the top of the world. Frozen inside one of the spheres was the most exquisite of specimens: a pure white dove that appeared to be suspended in time."

"Becca Hall!" cried Jalek, pleased with himself for making the connection.

"Patience, little one," said the old man. "One day, the wind seemed to swirl more rapidly than ever before. It seemed to whirl in a motion different from anything the people had ever experienced. It was as if the wind was being directed by a higher power. As it moved faster and faster, the large globe began to shake on the towering tree. It soon fell from its perch, tumbling down through the sky. As it fell to the ground, it landed on a soft drift of white powder."

"Snow," said Jalek.

"That's what you call it," replied the old man. "I'm not sure you'd be able to pronounce what we call it! In any case, seconds after the globe landed in the powder you call snow, things began to change. Suddenly, the drifts of ice melted, forming beautiful streams of mint water. Crystals made enchanting music as the water rushed through them. As the warmth spread, ribbons of color began to form and joined different regions of the kingdom. The trees of crystalized globes of glass turned into-"

"The setre trees!" cried Jalek.

"That's right, my friend. And there, far beyond the horizon, was the magical city of Gloriosa! Millions of years had passed. When the globe fell softly, not only did the dove trapped inside soar, but hidden within was a magical stone. It rolled down the ivory drifts. Soon it created the most majestic forest and waterfall ever seen."

"Wow, unbelievable!" said Jalek. "But that's not the end of the story, is it?"

Chapter 6 A Most Mysterious Time

Shaana opened her eyes to find herself lying on the ground with soaring trees looming above her. It was late evening, and she had fallen asleep. She stretched and decided to take a walk under the night sky. Strolling through the forest, she spotted a glimmer of light along the crystal stream. She couldn't identify the strange, glowing image and wondered what in the cosmos it could be. She rubbed her eyes in disbelief, wondering if perhaps she was still dreaming, but the image remained. She briefly considered running away in case this mysterious object proved dangerous, but instead decided to investigate.

There, sitting in the middle of the tallest setre tree, was a very strange looking little child. From a distance the child seemed very young, but as Shaana got closer she saw that the tiny person's features were that of an old woman. She wore a ragged cape over torn black trousers and a tattered white blouse.

"Who are you?" Shaana asked.

"You don't know me? I know who you are."

The mysterious one lifted her hand over Shaana's head. She began to chant hypnotically: "Close your eyes, close them and tell me what you see."

A jumble of thoughts tumbled through Shaana's mind. There were adventures from her youth and fleeting images from events that she couldn't remember clearly, events that she wasn't sure she wanted to remember at all.

"I do remember something," she admitted. "But not what, it's not what I expected to see."

"Those are sometimes the most important images of all. Keep going within," urged the curious person before her.

Shaana took a deep breath before continuing. "I see someone perched on the wings of the flying white horse. It's a young child, and the face I see is my own."

The old woman nodded, as if this was just what she'd expected to hear.

"Shaana, I am the spirit of what was once your great," the old woman began counting off on spindly fingers "great, great grandmother. I've watched over you throughout your entire young life." There were so many questions racing through Shaana's mind. She blurted out the one that may not be the most important, but for some reason felt like it most needed to be asked.

"What do you mean, 'what was once my great, great, great grandmother'? There were three 'greats', right, ma'am? She died years and years ago. How can you be here, talking with me like a real person?!"

"I am no longer part of your world, but as a spirit, I can still observe and sometimes even briefly assume a human form that allows me to talk with you, my dear."

"Oh, I see," Shaana said faintly, though she wasn't sure the old woman's explanation made things much clearer.

"You've grown up quite nicely. I'm quite glad to see you survived that awkward preteen stage, if you don't mind my saying so. You're now a beautiful young woman with a world of opportunity, but with that comes responsibility."

"And you're here to help me with that?" deduced Shaana. She knew she should be skeptical of this alleged spirit, but somehow she trusted her. When the woman suggested that they take a walk, Shaana found herself agreeing without hesitation.

As they strolled side by side through the kingdom, they started talking about Shaana's childhood and how she became queen. "Your parents were fine, wonderful people, Shaana."

"I know," Shaana said, though sometimes deep down she wondered.

"Your father was a great leader. And your mother was a most special woman, with the gift of making those around her better, happier people. You know the story. If it's too painful to..."

"No," Shaana said quickly, forgetting her usual impeccable manners by interrupting. "I'm ready to hear about it. I want to learn everything I can about--about what happened."

The old spirit woman nodded with understanding. "One day the kingdom began to rumble terribly. Your father stepped through the glowing waterfall and removed the magic stone from its resting place. And then--well, let me show you."

As Shaana took hold of her hand, she looked below and realized that they were floating just above the ground, slowly rising higher and higher until she could touch the very top of the tallest setre tree.

And suddenly, a scene unfolded below them that included the people Shaana loved most in the world. She saw her parents walking hand in hand across a colorway and into a forest. They soon came to a glowing waterfall and began to separate. Shaana's heart jumped in her throat: she wanted to tell them to stay together, to stay with her, but nothing she said could have altered the course of her family history, which the mysterious woman had somehow managed to capture and replay beneath them. Shaana noticed the regal Guardians of Time hovering near them. They were allowing her to find out the truth of what had happened to her parents, no matter how painful it might be. Her father reached for a stone and immediately disappeared into a portal, leading to a place that she couldn't see. Her mother's cries pierced Shaana's heart. This was the moment their lives had all been irreversibly altered.

"They didn't leave me deliberately," Shaana whispered. "My father didn't mean to disappear, and my mother spent her life searching for him, to reunite with him or at least make sure he was safe."

"They would never have abandoned you, my dear."

They continued to float high above the kingdom, over the colorways and throughout the cloudside. After they'd seen the entire kingdom from this new and lofty perspective, they slowly floated back down.

"How do you know all this? And how did you get the Guardians of Time to let me see it? And how..."

The woman gave her a gentle smile. "One question at a time, little one. I know all of this because Gloriasa is my home. My spirit has watched over this place for many, many years. As unbelievable as this may sound, my beloved husband is the one who discovered the magic of the stone and where to place it. We created this beautiful place. The kingdom you see before you is the realization of our greatest wishes and dreams."

"This place was your creation? That's wow!"

"I hope that you never stop allowing yourself to be 'wow'ed, little one."

"I've never felt like this before. I should be sad, but somehow I'm just relieved--happy, even. And, by the way, flying is every bit as fun as I thought it would be."

"I'm very glad to hear you say that. Remember, my dear, the more responsibilities you have, the more you need to have fun. It's important to stay happy and healthy, and you have a task ahead of you that may pose a challenge to that health and happiness."

"What do you mean?" asked Shaana, her euphoria giving way to nervousness.

"I've appeared to you now for a reason. You must help save our kingdom."

"But everything here is fine, isn't it?"

"There are some things I can't tell you, things you must discover on your own. Someone will come into your life. Someone who you must trust with all your heart."

As Shaana turned to gaze at the moon high in the night sky, she felt a gentle breeze.

"It's all so--wait, where are you? Where did you go? I have so many more questions! If you're my great, great, great grandmother who was my great, great, great grandfather?"

Shaana heard a now familiar voice faintly murmur the following words: "All in good time."

Chapter 7 The Old and The New

"My new friend, in order to truly appreciate Gloriosa, you must understand all its facets. This is my favorite part," said the Ancient One.

From behind the castle walls, music flowed through the air. A flute chirped sweetly, like a baby bird perched on a branch. The vibrating strings of a violin, the cascade of a viola, the foundation of a cello all seamlessly played together. Suddenly, the tempo accelerated to a maddening pace. At first the notes turned dramatic, almost dark. Then they shifted to sounds that were oh so sweet. The people were all smiles, even the flurbur seemed to be smiling. Their wings beat steadily along with the music. Globes danced on the colorway, literally bouncing to the music. In the center of all this music-inspired activity stood Recima, Gaba and of course Shaana.

Off in the distance on the edge of the most vibrant colorway sat Teragil. A tear rolled slowly down his cheek as he remembered the past, reflected on the present, and looked into the future. He found himself hoping that everything could remain as perfect as it was at that very moment, even knowing that that was an impossible dream. Without warning, the sound of the flute returned. Ribbons of color stretched in every direction, almost touching the castle walls. The sky was filled with stars. There, by his side as always, stood Becca Hall.

Teragil began to tell Jalek another tale of long ago.

"On the far side of Gloriosa, next to the farthest colorway, round objects floated around in space. We called them Zlasgru."

"Huh?" said Jalek.

"You heard me, Zlasgru! The people who lived in this untouched oasis had something very special. The little village was nestled between gigantic mountains in the midst of a beautiful valley. The village was centered around a beautiful body of crystal clear water, so translucent that it was like a magical reflection. This is where Recima and Gaba were born. They lived on the side of the mountain overlooking the lake.

As young children, the two of them would sit on the side of the mountain and watch the wonders of their world. When they were old enough, they would sit on the wings of a Neswa, a pristine white bird. The Neswa would fly them all around the lake. Sometimes the Neswa would float right on the water, and other times it would fly just above it. As you would say, Jalek, it was very 'cool'!

When they got older, they would play a game where each one would get on the back of a different Neswa and they would race across the lake as fast as posisble."

"Now that's cool," said Jalek.

"I knew you would think that," Teragil said, and they exchanged a smile. Jalek had never had this much fun with an adult before. For his part, Teragil was delighted by Jalek's spirit.

"So what do you think, Jalek?"

"Think about what?"

"Do you want to try flying on a Neswa?"

"Could we?" said Jalek, jumping eagerly to his feet.

"Before we go, I must tell you this--when Gaba and Recima were very young, there lived an evil man in the remote part of Gloriosa. His name was Thiler, and he was the only evil person in all of Gloriosa. You see, years earlier Kier had banished Thiler's father from all of the kingdom and sent him to the Frozen Zone. Like his father before him, Thiler's goal was a simple one. He planned to start by taking over the little part of Gloriosa he knew best, and then slowly but surely conquer the rest of Gloriosa. Those who did not follow would either be relegated to isolation or disposed of. His followers were strange beings indeed, with oddly shaped faces and bodies and extremely long tentacles. With a slight turn, crystals would fly from their tentacles in all directions, killing everything in the vicinity. He built a small fortress where he kept the property he and his followers had stolen from the people of the kingdom, including all of their most sacred belongings.

One night when the sky was at its very darkest, Thiler kidnapped Gaba and Recima's parents. He had discovered that they were close to sending him into oblivion. They had uncovered his plan to take over their kingdom bit by bit. Needless to say, Thiler was not about to let someone thwart his evil plans and decided to get rid of these obstacles the only way he knew how. As he was dragging Gaba and Recima's parents forcibly out of their home, the children woke. They tried to stop him, but they lacked the skills

and strength. They never saw their parents again. And their last memory of their parents was of their terrified faces as this evil man laughingly took them away. As you might imagine, this has haunted them their entire lives."

"That's terrible," said Jalek. "Is there anything we can do? Hey, is there some way the Sprited Ones could help?"

"You see, my young friend, it was Kier who finally defeated this malicious, power-hungry, evil man. In fact, that's how Kier became king; the people were so highly grateful that he had restored peace to the kingdom. No matter how busy he was ruling the kingdom, Kier always had time for Recima and Gaba, and cared for them as if they were his own."

Pondering for a moment, Jalek reached a sudden but clear conclusion: the way to help Recima and Gaba would be for them to come on the adventure with him and the Sprited Ones. They had been powerless before, but this would be their chance to regain faith in themselves and try to finally get justice for what happened that fateful night.

Chapter 8 Dreamscape

Jalek awoke in the middle of the night, feeling frightened and confused. Looking around, he was relieved to find himself in his own bed. There was no old man in sight, just his beloved posters and sports momentos. He rubbed the sleep from his eyes, got out of bed and cautiously walked downstairs. At the bottom of the stairs, he noticed a light through the window. He looked up and there in the night sky beyond the moon, he saw what he thought he had dreamed: a flicker of light.

A kingdom? Could it be Gloriosa?

"You must find a way to save us," whispered a mysterious voice. Jalek knew that the voice must be Teragil's. Thoughts tumbled through his sleep-deprived mind: had he really been there or had it been a very vivid dream? And if this were a real world filled with real people who needed help, what could he do to save them?

"Indeed, my young friend," he heard the Ancient One say, responding to his questions even though Jalek had not asked them out loud. "We have much work to do."

The boy recalled the story the old man had told. He started to better understand the tale of the three kingdoms, the games the kids play, the musical streams. He smiled as he remembered the white horses flying around the edge of the kingdom. In his dreams, he began to understand. He could help save Polara, even if he wasn't yet sure how to do it or who to turn to for help. Outside his window, the clouds around the distant mountaintops lifted.

Suddenly, Jalek noticed massive robotic figures rising from the water. He felt oddly reassured by their presence, recalling that they were there to protect the colorways of time. With a sudden sense of certainty, Jalek realized the colorways were the way to bring the kingdoms back together. Within seconds, Jalek found himself flying through the air. He had the odd but thrilling experience of watching himself soaring through this new world. There he was playing Cometball!

Wow, this was great,' he thought. 'Much more fun than soccer, and you can't--ouch!'

All of a sudden, Jalek found himself flat on his bottom.

Beside him, Teragil was smiling, amused the boy had figured out the game was not as easy as it may have appeared. Jalek got up with only his ego bruised, and he and Teragil began to walk. Soon they had reached the center of Gloriosa. As he recalled the stories the old man had told, he found himself sitting by the musical streams. Contrary to his expectations, it wasn't noisy at all. He wanted to see more.

In the blink of an eye, he was standing on the ribbons of color. "What's that?" he asked excitedly. Through the clouds in the distance, they spotted a grand but somehow not intimidating statue.

"Do you see the movement there?" Teragil asked. "Currents of time flow around her in every direction."

Jalek stared for a moment before asking two of the many questions that sprung to mind. "How do you choose the right direction? And how is it that you can move through time?"

"I know you desire answers," replied Teragil sympathetically. "But remember where you are; things here are not easily explained, but there is always a resolution. When you most need to travel through time, that's when the currents will appear."

The next thing he knew, Teragil was urging him to hold on. "Your sense of adventure will help with the challenges to come. And remember that you can help The Spirited Ones, so don't allow yourself to doubt that, no matter what happens."

"But I don't know how to find them!" cried Jalek. "Can you?"

"I can't, my young friend," said the old man regretfully. "You must find them yourself."

Suddenly he was tumbling farther down, once again landing on his well-worn bottom. Even as he spun, he thought he saw three human figures through the rays of color. It couldn't be, though, because what would three children be doing there? And by the time Jalek had once again endured a harsh landing on the ground below, they were gone.

"I'm spending a lot of time down here," muttered the boy.

He looked up to find the person whom he knew without a doubt was Becca Hall.

"Follow me," she ordered, in a voice that was brusque but not unkind.

"But I can't fly!" Jalek protested.

"Oh, really? Haven't gotten that down yet, have you? Well, never mind then. I'll fly slowly and you can walk beneath me."

She took him through the Frozen Zone. He saw the frozibs, but instead of them soaring upwards as he'd expected, they dipped down into the lake. The water began to bubble, and suddenly a Crewat rose from the lake. The creature spun around and took possession of the Spirited Ones. He roared, clearly in a fury for reasons only he could understand. His limbs flailed wildly around in every possible direction.

"There's nothing to worry about," shouted Albee, trying to sound like he meant it. Azeal defiantly challenged the beast to come after her and leave the others alone.

Before the enraged creature could take her up on the offer, Rezak offered some calming words: "I know that we can beat him. All we have to do is stay together."

Jalek believed that, too, but he also feared it would be easier said than done.

Chapter 9 Trust Your Instincts

Suspended in time, he couldn't see the sights around him. Everything was blurry. Suddenly, through the haze, Jalek heard a familiar voice: "Remember, we have much work to do. You must use your imagination and your faith in others."

"Where are you?" Jalek asked nervously, not filled with any self-confidence at all. "I can't see you!"

Teragil's voice was calming. "You will not always be able to see me, my young friend--but I will always be with you."

"I'm just not sure what you want me to do."

"To discover what to do on the outside, find the answers inside. I will always help you, even if it's not in the ways you expect."

"But I still don't understand exactly how to help them." His own sentence was interrupted by a thud. Falling hard by the side of the lake, he began to realize where he was and to focus on what he was seeing. Oh, no! The Spirited Ones! The menacing Crewat had gotten hold of them!

Thinking quickly, he grabbed the white powder from the ground, molded it into a ball and threw it at the creature in an attempt to distract it from his frightened pris-oners. At first, his efforts failed. When he tried again, the Crewat slowly turned and started directly toward him. Jalek started to run, going at a speed he didn't know he was capable of reaching.

"Help!" Jalek wasn't sure whether he said the word aloud, but he sure knew that's what he was thinking. Then Jalek grabbed the glass ball hanging off the tree and threw it at the creature with all his might. B o o m ! With a sudden explosion, the globe burst open to engulf the creature. Jalek and the four children he knew were The Spirited Ones looked up to find that the Crewat was now trapped within the crystalized ball.

"How did you do that?" asked Azeal, with a mixture of admiration and wariness. After all, just as their world was new and exotic to Jalek, to them he was an outsider whose intentions, traits and abilities were still unknown.

"I don't know how I did it," he said truthfully. "And if it's what I think it is, your're gonna think I'm crazy."

"No, tell us," they urged.

"Well, I closed my eyes and made myself believe that this would work and somehow it did. It was just my imagination, but I kind of made it become reality, like the Ancient One told me I would."

"The who said what?" asked Albee.

"Who is the Ancient One? And, as long as we're on the subject, who are you?"

"I don't know exactly who the Ancient One is, but I do know his name is Teragil. As for me, my name's Jalek. But feel free to just refer to me as the guy who saved you!"

He said this last part with a smile, and they immediately smiled back. Somehow, Jalek knew at that moment that they would get along. He took a minute to appraise them one by one.

Albee had a tough exterior that Jalek sensed hid a kind and generous nature. Rezak was the type of person who didn't speak that often, but when he did, everyone immediately listened to what he had to say. And Azeal had a daring, risk-taking quality that Jalek admired and hoped he, too, might possess.

Far off in the distance, Becca Hall and Teragil observed their young charges.

"I told you so," said Becca Hall, unable to resist.

"You only told me what I already knew," Teragil replied. "I knew he would believe. That's why I chose him. And when he and the Spirited Ones join forces, they just might be able to save our world."

Chapter 10 Together

Jalek rose and began to brush himself off. The Spirited Ones followed his lead.

"Are you ok, Albee?" asked Jalek. "How about you guys, Azeal, Rezak?"

Azeal started to politely respond and then interrupted herself. "Wait a minute! How do you know our names? Where are you from?"

"Yeah!" piped up Albee, never one to restrain his curiosity in favor of courtesy. "There are a whole bunch of questions you still haven't answered!"

"Well, sometimes you don't know how you know things, you just do," said Jalek, feeling he was starting to sound a little like Teragil. "I know from the stories I was told that they call you the Spirited Ones, right? Oh, and I remember some other stuff, too."

Jalek began to tell them the story that the Ancient One had so recently told him. He tried to explain what had happened to the three kingdoms and to describe them all, especially Gloriosa.

"I've heard of Gloriosa," said Azeal. "Only I thought it was just a make believe place."

"Well, what's the second kingdom?" asked Albee.

"Polara," replied Jalek, surprised at how much he remembered of what Teragil had shared with him.

"Oh, yeah, well that's where we live. We already know all about that one!"

"So then I guess you know that right now we're in a part of Polara called The Frozen Zone, only, well, its not frozen right here, is it?"

"How come?"

They all seemed to look to Jalek for answers, but he wasn't sure whether he could give them. "I don't know, but the Ancient One told me that certain things around here just can't be explained, at least not right away."

"You can say that again," remarked Albee.

"So what do we do now?" asked Azeal.

"Oh, nothing too drastic, just a little time travel," Jalek said with a smile.

"What's so little about that?" cried Albee. "But wait, actually-"

"Wait for what?" asked Rezak.

"Of course!" said Azeal.

"What?" asked Rezak again. "Oh!" The meaning had magically become clear.

Jalek looked from one to the other and thought about how cool it was that they always seemed to understand one another without even speaking. He wondered whether he would ever have that type of connection with someone. For now, though, he had more pressing worries at hand.

The words "You must believe...", both comforting and ominous, echoed faintly through the silence.

Chapter 11 Back in Time

Albee wandered off alone for a moment.

"What's wrong?" asked Jalek, following him.

"I'm scared," Albee admitted. The swag he usually had seemed to be fading away. "The others don't think I get afraid, but I do."

"We're all scared," Jalek said comfortingly. "But being scared isn't enough of a reason not to do the stuff you're supposed to do."

As Jalek and the Spirited Ones pondered what do next, Teragil and Becca Hall were trying to formulate a plan of their own. Well, at least Becca Hall was.

"We must get them through the Frozen Zone and back to the portal," insisted Becca Hall.

"Patience, my flying friend! They must learn to trust their own instincts and make their own choices."

"I hate it when you're right, old man," she grumbled.

"I prefer to be called the Ancient One."

"Yeah, sure, whatever. Listen, how about we give them just a tiny bit of help? I've got this idea."

Azeal, trusting her instincts, told the others to close their eyes. "Imagine where it is we came from. Relax and focus. There can't be any room for doubt!"

As they opened their eyes, it was there as clear as could be: an illuminated pathway. They stared at each other for a moment, as if to confirm that they were all seeing the same thing, and began to walk along the pathway.

Flying high above, the Frozibs soared through the swirling blizzard and skillfully dodged the slivers of ice. Some of the Frozibs landed on the tall trees while others disappeared into the soft white powder below.

"Remember," said Jalek, "we must use our imaginations! If we do, the Frozibs won't be able to hurt us."

Almost at the exact same instant, they spotted Becca Hall and began running towards her. They came to the base of a frozen white drift. The remnants of the now missing stone radiated a faint glow.

"We can't climb! It's too steep!"

"We don't have to climb," said Jalek, struck by a sudden inspiration. He reached for the Spirited Ones. As they all joined hands, they began to float above the towering drift all the way to the top.

"Good use of your imagination," came an approving voice from above.

"Teragil! I knew you would be here with us."

"In one way or another," he agreed. "Now, just close your eyes. That's right, all of you! And now you can take the last step."

As they closed their eyes and stepped forward, they found themselves on the other side of the waterfall. It took them a few moments to realize they'd arrived back in Polara.

"What does all this mean?" asked Albee.

"I think," said Rezak, who'd finally started to understand, "that we must go back in time."

"Why?" yelled Albee. This was not exactly the kind of thing they were used to doing.

"I think, well, the only way to change the future is to alter the past," offered Jalek.

"Remember the story of Kier?" said Azeal. "What if we could travel back in time and keep Kier from grabbing the stone? Then Polara won't ever separate from Gloriosa."

"But that also means the rest of the past and future will change," observed Rezak. "What will happen to us? What if, like, there isn't an 'us' in this new future?"

"I'm not sure," admitted Jalek. "But if I had to take a guess, I'd say I'm here to help things work out like they're meant to...not that we know exactly what that is yet."

Teragil and Becca Hall, watching anxiously from above, nodded in approval.

The wind began to swirl. The Spirited Ones exchanged looks of nervous excitement and once again joined hands. They whispered reminders to one another and themselves to believe. Becca Hall circled around them faster and faster, surrounding them in a bubble of glass. Suddenly, they were traveling through currents of time. Streaks of red and blue rushed past them and they experienced a mass explosion of lights and color.

"How do we know when to stop?" asked Albee breathlessly.

"Don't worry. We'll stop when it's time."

Chapter 12 A New Beginning

For a moment, the children were unaware of what was happening around them. The dizzying speed at which they were being propelled through space didn't allow for much thought or conversation, and it was only when they all came to a sudden halt that they focused on their surroundings. They were mesmerized by what they saw in the distance: a majestic spectrum of color that served as a gateway to a place that they all instinctively knew was an entirely new world.

They all began talking at once, speaking in sentence fragments since they were too astonished to formulate full sentences: "So here we are, a new place. Maybe even a new time?" "But where is here?" "I'm not sure, but we're--how did that happen?"
"Oh, my! "

Suddenly, Jalek gasped.

"Look! Over there by the falling water! Is that Kier? And the woman with him, is that Tala? This must be Gloriosa! Do you think they can they see us? Can they hear us talking?"

"I'm not sure," replied Rezak, never wanting to jump to the wrong conclusion.

"I'm sure they can't see or hear us," said Azeal, who didn't share Rezak's concern.

"It's as amazing as Teragil said it would be," said Jalek, wanting to take a moment to enjoy it.

"It's incredible," agreed Albee. "And look above the clouds. There's a castle, just like the ones you hear about in faily tales!"

Jalek, feeling a little like a tour guide even though he'd never been there before, pointed out the colorways, the towering melaph trees with those musical liquid leaves that swayed in the breeze and the glowing birds that he remembered were called flurbur. Teragil had described this magical place so vividly that he felt oddly comfortable there despite never actually having seen it before.

"We have to find Gaba, Recima, and Queen Shaana." Jalek paused. "Wait a minute. She wouldn't be a queen, though, right? Not if we're now in the past."

"I'm so confused," admitted Rezak.

"Let's not forget why we're here," said the ever practical Azeal. "We need to convince Kier not to reach for the magic stone."

"Maybe instead of trying to stop him from getting the stone, we could make them choose a different colorway," suggested Rezak.

"Oh, yeah, that's much easier," Albee said sarcastically.

"What if we could somehow make them see us," Rezak continued, refusing to let his friend's jokes get to him.

"Or at least hear us." added Azeal.

"Maybe we could distract them, and get them to follow us."

"Follow us where?" asked Albee.

"Anywhere," murmured Jalek. "There must be some way to do this. I know it's not impossible."

At that moment, Becca Hall and Teragil appeared at the crest of the colorway.

"You're here!" Jalek said gratefully. He smiled rather triumphantly at his new friends. "See, I told you he was real!"

Teragil looked at each child in turn. "This may be the greatest test of all. You have all done magnificently so far, but you must use every ounce of imagination that you possess to accomplish the task at hand. Each of you will have to find determination that you may not even believe you have."

Jalek knew by now that Teragil wasn't going to give him any direct answers, but he still felt more confident just knowing he was there.

"Okay, everyone, let's think for a minute. Tala and Kier would definitely follow their daughter, wouldn't they? So let's say we could get Shaana to lead them away from that particular colorway. Kier would never be tempted to grab the stone in the first place, because he'd never see the waterfall and the glow behind it. Then everything would work out like it's meant to!"

"You're a genius," declared Albee, never one to refrain from effusive praise of others or, for that matter, himself.

"Yeah, well, my teachers never thought so," muttered Jalek, pleased but embarrassed by the compliment. "Besides, we still have to convince Shaana, Recima, and Gaba to help. As of now, they can't even see or hear us!"

"So our first task is to find them," Azeal pointed out.

"Let's head for the castle," suggested Jalek. "Where else would the daughter of a king and queen be?"

They made their way through Gloriosa, amazed that some people actually lived their daily lives in this magical place as casually and comfortably as they did in their own homelands. "I can't believe it. We're actually walking on a colorway!"

"And it's so simple," Azeal said confidently. "Each one joins another cloud. Oops! Okay. Maybe it's not that simple."

Hearing the sound of the musical stream, Jalek knelt beside it and took a drink. "Mint," he said appreciatively.

"But not the kind of mint that reminds me of toothpaste. It's delicious!"

As they stopped to sample the mint-flavored stream, they spotted a beautiful young girl at the base of the next colorway. Golden brown hair shimmered to her fingertips, and her eyes were like glistening emeralds. Without even knowing them, she greeted them with a warm smile. She leaned forward with a graceful nod, her hands palm to palm just beneath her chin. Jalek had never been greeted that way, but somehow it seemed more welcoming than a simple hello.

Jalek knew instinctively that he was staring right at Shaana. "I think that's..."

"We know!" they replied.

"What should we say to her?"

"How about hello," Albee suggested dryly.

"I'll go with you," offered Rezak.

Jalek took a deep breath and ventured over. "Hi! My name is..."

"His name is Jalek," Rezak supplied helpfully.

Jalek was taken aback by a strong feeling that he couldn't quite identify. He knew it wasn't a romantic connection that he sensed, but yet he couldn't shake the feeling that he was connected to this girl in some important way. Thankfully, he was saved from having to talk to her on his own because Azeal and Albee came up beside him just as Recima and Gaba joined Shaana.

"We're going to tell you some things that might sound a little--well, crazy. But just hear us out and keep an open mind."

Jalek, with the help of his three young friends, began telling Shaana, Recima, and Gaba all they knew about why they were there and what should be done to save the king-doms.

"So you're from the future and are here to change the course of history?" Recima said. "Not something I hear every day."

Jalek turned to look directly at Recima and Gaba. "I know the story of your child-hood. I know this sounds weird, but if you help us, I think you'll end up helping yourselves as well."

"It does sound weird," agreed Recima.

Jalek shifted uncomfortably from one foot to the other. "I just meant that--well, maybe there's nothing you can do to change what happened to your own family, but you can help someone else reunite with theirs. There are no guarantees, but isn't it always better to at least try?"

Gaba turned to the future queen. "What do you think, Shaana?"

Shaana looked surprised by her own reply. "I, I think I believe them. And, besides, someone told me you were coming."

"Huh?" said Jalek, but before Shaana could reply, he reminded the group that time was of the essence. He filled Shaana, Gaba, and Recima in on their plan: "The key is that we have to keep Kier and Tala away from the colorway that leads to the waterfall."

"I think I saw them go this way," said Gaba, and they all started running as fast as they could. They came to a clump of beautiful green trees, surrounded by flowers of every conceivable color. As they slowed down to catch their breath, they caught a glimpse of two people walking on a colorway in the distance. The two were heading toward a majestic cascade of falling water illuminated by a radiant glow.

"We have to hurry," said Jalek, his heart galloping in his chest.

Desperate to save the couple and the future of the kingdoms, Shaana scrambled to the top of the cloud.

Just as Recima reached Kier, Shaana slipped off the edge and began tumbling down through the layers of clouds. Kier heard her cries of distress and leapt from colorway to colorway until he was closer to the girl who, unbeknownst to him, would one day become the queen. He realized with frustration that no matter how quickly he moved, it wasn't quite fast enough to catch up with the frightened girl, who was still falling through the clouds.

Gaba and Recima glanced at each other, and then leapt on to the nearest Newswa before they could talk themselves out of it. Kier looked understandably mystified by what the two children were doing and how they seemed to be flying independently through the air. Newswas were creatures that could only be seen and used by children. After circling around to no avail, they finally reached Shaana and pulled her onto the Newswa. Shaana had time to give them each a grateful hug before they brought her back to Kier. She leapt into her father's arms, who looked delighted but still confused by all that had transpired.

Tala ran toward her husband. "Kier! I saw you fall! And why were you running? I was so scared. Are you okay? Tell me you're okay enough to hear me yell at you for running away from me!"

Shaana caught up with Jalek just before he and the Spirited Ones disappeared from sight.

"How did you know we would catch you?" asked Jalek.

"I didn't know for certain," Shaana admitted. "But I knew I had to trust my instincts and just believe it would turn out for the best."

"Well, your instincts are obviously pretty good," Jalek told her.

"They're telling me something else, too," Shaana said. "I know people keep asking who you are, and I think this might be the right time to give you part of that answer."

"Go on," Jalek said, feeling an anxious flutter in his stomach.

"You and I, we're linked by more than just the adventures we had today. I think we're related."

Chapter 13 Back to the Beginning

"We must go back," said the ever-practical Azeal.

They said goodbye and joked about how they all had this feeling they'd see one another sometime in the future.

"So now what?" asked Albee.

"Maybe we should ask them," said Jalek, pointing upwards.

There on the colorway stood Becca Hall and Teragil, gazing proudly at their young charges. Becca Hall favored them with a quick wink.

"First we go back to where we're supposed to be," declared Teragil with a smile.

Suddenly, the wind began to swirl. Becca Hall circled around them with increasing speed until a bubble of glass had formed. Once again, they were traveling through currents of time. While the first time they had felt afraid, this time they experienced only excitement.

As they moved faster and faster through space, they could see only streaks of red and orange light. When the bubble at last began to decrease its frenetic pace, the sights around them become clearer.

"Where are we?" asked Albee.

The others joined in with questions of their own: "Since we prevented Kier from picking up the magic stone, does Polara even exist?" "Do we have a home to go to? Where will we end up?" "Will Shaana and Kier remember what happened when we see them in the future?"

"I don't know," Jalek admitted, "but I guess we're about to find out!" He noticed he felt less worried than he used to about not knowing the answers to his questions.

"This isn't the Polara we left," Azeal noted, taking a careful look around. "It looks sort of like Polara, but different."

"Well, thanks for clearing that up," joked Albee.

Rezak giggled. "Azeal's right. Like, for example, I know this tree. Look, these are my initials! But it looks a little different than it did before. And since when do we have ribbons of color in Polara?"

They all figured it out at the same time. The formerly grim Polara was now Gloriosa! The kingdoms had been unified, and Polara had taken on the vibrancy and joy that previously only inhbitants of Gloriosa had been able to enjoy.

They took a moment to enjoy their new and improved home. Overhead, white horses galloped through the sky. And there in the distance stood Becca Hall and Teragil, a radiant mist of color behind them. They stopped at the edge of the stream. As the gates opened, they were greeted with a scene of fluffy white trees lining a cobblestone path. They heard the voices of the flurburs perched on the tree and felt a gentle breeze blowing through the air.

"Let's find Shaana," suggested Jalek. "I can't wait to see how it all turned out."

Their search for Shaana took them on a quick tour of the new Polara, which they now guessed was called Gloriosa. Other people seemed as pleased with the changes as they were, laughing, listening to the music in the air and even playing a spirited game of fabasclou.

They soon found Shaana, who was happily beholding the changed world before her. She, Gaba and Recima stood waving happily to the happy subjects of their kingdom, who were waving back in-between games of Fabasclou and munching on fruit from the setre trees.

She smiled at their approach, and they all greeted each other with the gentle bow that Shaana had introduced them to. "Thank you for saving our world. I hope you realize how much good you've done."

"Thanks," Jalek murmured, feeling suddenly shy. He seemed to feel that way a lot around Shaana.

"Where are you from?" she asked. "And do you think--will we ever see you again?"

"I hope so," Jalek said. "I guess it's time for me to go home, but right now I'm not even sure where that is or if it'll be the same place I left."

"But isn't your home here with us now?" asked Albee.

Jalek smiled. "I have a feeling I'll be back here some day. Maybe even on another adventure."

As you're already discovering, my young friend, anything is possible if you believe." Teragil appeared with a smile and an outstretched hand, ready to guide his young charge home. "Remember all I have told you and that there are still many more stories to tell.

"So this place is real?" Jalek asked.

He took a moment to take in these magical surroundings for what he suddenly feared was the last time: the sky that was bluer than it was back home, soft arches of color visible as far as they eye could see, statuesque figures standing proud and tall.

Chapter 13 One Last Story

Jalek awoke in his own bedroom. He rubbed the sleep from his eyes and climbed slowly out of bed, feeling confused and a little disoriented. After all, it's not like he traveled through time to other kingdoms every day.

Fragments of the stories that Teragil had told swirled through his mind. He wasn't sure which parts of these stories, if any, he'd just experienced in reality. He lay back down on his bed. Maybe he just needed more sleep. Didn't people always say that lack of sleep could make you crazy?

Drifting in and out of wakefulness, he heard the Ancient One's voice: "We have much work to do, my young friend."

"We're almost there," announced a familiar voice.

It was his mother. Jalek, now fully awake, looked around to find himself in the back seat of their Toyota. "Time to wake up," his mother said, glancing at him in the rearview mirror.

He turned toward the window just in time to catch the name of the street they were turning onto: Gloriosa Lane.

"What the..."

"What's wrong?" asked his mother. She sounded tired.

"It's just--I didn't know this was Gloriosa Lane," Jalek said, unable to explain.

"That's right," she said, just a touch impatiently.

"Mount Polara cemetery is located at the end of Gloriosa Lane."

"But..." Jalek trailed off.

Moments later, they found themselves in front of the tombstone for the service.

"Here rests the beloved Gilbert Terry. His friends called him Teragil:
'The greatest storyteller of all time.'

Here rests the beloved
Gilbert Terry

His friends called him:

"Teragil,
The greatest storyteller of
all time."

Always by my side

Colorways

"Story tellers" are a marvelous breed.

Colorways tells the story of young boy named Jalek who embraces the tales told by the "Ancient One," Teragil.

A wonderful journey of adventure, determination, pride and most of all, understanding that profound power is control of your own mind. If you believe, anything is possible.

You will thoroughly enjoy this adventure as we travel to magical and mysterious places, and grow to understand that each of us needs all of us.